PRETTY SNEAKY

by

Don Alan

First Edition: 1956
.Second Printing: 1960
Third Printing: 1968
Fourth Printing: 1973

Fifth printing, 1975

Sixth printing, 1977

Reprinted, 1982

Published by

MAGIC, INC.

5082 N. Lincoln Av.,
Chicago, Ill. 60625

Marianna Gava, (Miss Illinois); Hugh Hefner, Editor
& Publisher of Playboy; and Don Alan, Pretty Sneaky
Magician on the Playboy TV Show, December 1959.

✹✹✹

Dedicated to all my sneaky friends -----

For without them, I'd be a total stranger.

Don Alan

2

INDEX

ABOUT DON ALAN

"Close Up Time" , Don Alan's first book, and "Pretty Sneaky" were written at the time Don was involin his own TV shows (he had several), and he was loaded with inventive ideas. He is still a very clever performer, but now that he has a world wide reputation, is one of the top names in magic, has a family to manage - he doesn't have the time for book writing. Which is our loss.

Don's TV career began in 1952 with his first show, each one of the 26 showings featuring another top magician besides Don. This format was used in several Don Alan shows, giving work to many performers.

Don was born in 1926 in Norwood, Ohio. He was in Special Services during World War II, and following that, was a student at the Chavez School. His background of television in the early years of his career has earned him many fine engagements in every part of this country and England. In recent years, he has been busy with trade show work.

Among magicians, he is a popular lecturer and one of our most knowledgeable conjurers. One day we hope he will have the time to work on a long proposed book. Meanwhile, the material in those now on the market is still fresh and very usable – very Don Alan.

THE FOUR JACKS AND THE BOUNCING BALL

Effect: The performer shuffles the four jacks into the pack. Upon riffling the pack, the performer boasts that the four jacks are in his pocket. From his pocket he removes the four jacks, children's variety, and rolls them onto the table. After the laughter subsides (maybe) the performer spreads the pack face up on the table and slowly removes the four jacks (card type) from his pocket. Heh! Heh!

Preparation: Secure four toy jacks and the usual small rubber ball, and place these into your right coat pocket. Also beg, borrow or as a last resort, buy a deck of playing cards. You are now ready.

To Perform: Grit your teeth and remove the four jacks from the pack. Fan the pack face up and place the four jacks into different parts of the pack. Square up pack and perform the Multiple Shift (see Tarbell Vol. 3, page 192.) This will bring the four jacks to the top of the pack when it is turned face down. Holding the pack in your left hand, secure a break under the four jacks, by anybody's favorite method.

Hold this with the tip of your left little finger. Boldly assert that the four jacks are now in your pocket. Turn your right side toward the spectator (s) and with your right hand reach in and remove the four toy jacks.

While you are doing this your left hand quietly drops the four jacks into your left coat pocket. This may or may not be a principle in misdirection. The right hand in the meantime has rolled the four toy jacks onto the table.

After the disgusted look on the spectator's face has disappeared, spread the pack face up on the table, show your left hand empty and reach into the left coat pocket and remove the four regular jacks. The right hand now removes from your pocket the small red ball, bounces same, and with one clean sweep picks up the four jacks in one motion before the ball comes down. (This last move may be gotten from any sneaky little kid in your neighborhood.) The ball and jacks are then put into the right coat pocket and you are finished. And maybe you are..............

SNEAKY CARD TO POCKET   HOW ELSE?

Here is a sneaky routine with two selected cards.

Preparation: Place a " Card in the Wallet" or " Card in the Envelope" gimmick into your left breast pocket of your coat. I use Le Paul's excellent gimmick (See Le Paul's Card Magic, page 214.) Also place the familiar Insurance Policy trick into the same pocket, but on the outside of the gimmick already there. Also you will need a pack of cards and a marking pencil.

To Perform: First force the card matching your Insurance Policy, and then have a second card selected. Whatever method you use, make sure that both cards are selected in the same manner. Have both cards marked and returned to the deck.

You now have only to control the freely selected card to the top of the pack.   Explain that you will attempt to find the first card behind your back. Place pack behind you and immediately palm the top card, which is the second selected card, in your right hand.

Then turn the next card on the top of the pack face up and bring pack to the front, holding it in your left hand, so that the spectators may see the face up card. Ask if the face up card is one of the selected cards. When the answer is " no " , immediately reach into the left breast pocket with your right hand, loading palmed card into gimmick.

At the same time remove Insurance Policy and explain that you have insurance on failures. Replace policy and state that the policy gives you two chances. Once again place pack behind your back and turn another card face up on the pack and bring forward, asking if this is one of the selected cards.

When they say " no" again, ask the name of the first selected card. When you receive the name of the card, explain that THAT CARD happens to be the only card not covered on the policy. State that they have a whole clause on it and unfold the policy, as in the usual routine.

Now fold and replace the policy and say that you will try to find the second selected card. Once again you

6

fail and explain: "That's what I like about insurance. They have so many clauses."

Reach in and remove the envelope gimmick, stating that you just received additional coverage. Tear off the end of the envelope and have spectator remove selected card. (nas pas)

Notes: This idea was worked out while working a convention under the worst conditions imaginable, only there I did the dirty work under the table. Use either method as the occasion demands. The two tricks combined give each other a reason, which I think is most important in any presentation. If your suit (s) does not have breast pockets on the left side, merely reverse the handling or the coat.

- - - - -

"I' LL FIND IT WITH MY SLIDE RULE"

Effect: A selected card is found by using a slide rule, in a routine strictly for laffs. Sort of a much to do about nothing.

Preparation: Secure a small 6" slide rule at a stationary shop. Then take a Jumbo card and cut out one index. This will measure 1/2 x 1 1/2", see figure 1. A miniature card could be used, but I' ve found the jumbo pip far superior as all can see it easily.

Now glue this onto the sliding section of the slide rule on the underneath side. Place slide rule in pocket so that you can remove it, without exposing the underneath side.

Fig.1   To perform: Take your trusty packet of cards and force the five of spades. This matches your Jumbo pip on the slide rule. Have spectator look at card and then instruct him to place card face down in front of him. Explain that you will find the identity of his card by calculation. Remove slide rule and say: "Now I' ll have to ask you a few questions, so as to calculate your card. Is your card red or black?"

(Upon receiving all the answers to the following questions, move your slide rule as if figuring out a problem).

Is your card a spade or a club (move slide). Is your card a picture card or a number card (move rule). Is your number card an even number or an odd number (move rule). Now is your odd number between 1 and 6 or 6 and 10 (move slide). Now you see by asking just a few leading questions I can practically tell you the name of your card - all by following this little line. Of course you have to follow it around to the other side (here you turn rule over, exposing the Jumbo pip.)

Explain: " The reason they put this on here is because most people don't know how to read slide rules, and I am one of them."

Now have spectator turn his card over to verify same. By having spectator keep his card in front of him, you are protected. I have often found these laymen to be " Pretty Sneaky."

— — — — — —

THE IMPROMPTU CARD ON THE WALL

In my book "Close Up Time" (we still have a few copies left) I described a method for doing the card on the wall. But it has two drawbacks. First, the card must be a duplicate, and second, the card cannot be marked by the spectator. Here is a method given to me by my sneaky friend, Howard Bamman of Chicago. This is an impromptu method, using only one tack.

Preparation: Borrow a tack from the spectator. This may not be easy, so if he has deliberately left his tack at home, produce some of your own. These may be carried easily by sticking a few into a small cork ball. Also you will need a rubber band, a marking pencil, and a pack of cards. These are all placed on the table. Now you are ready........

To perform: Have a card selected and marked by the spectator. Have the card returned to the pack and control it to the bottom of the pack. Now take the rubber band and circle the narrow side of the pack twice. See the illustration. The tack is now placed point up between the bands, which form sort of a rail to hold the tack.

You are now almost set to do the dirty work. Ask the spectator to name his card, and as he does, turn away, stealing the selected card from the bottom of the pack (a la color changing move) and place it on the top of the pack, so that the tack pierces the card.

You then throw the pack against the wall or ceiling, and the selected card will be seen, and the pack will fall to the floor neatly, due to the rubber band.

Note: The stealing of the selected card from the bottom of the pack takes just a few seconds. This whole operation should be done as you turn from the spectator to throw the pack. Try this and you'll find it's Pretty Sneaky.

- - - - - -

"WOT HOPPENED?"

Effect: Two cards are displayed on the table. One card is placed into the performer's pocket. The two cards then change places. This looks like real magic, pretty sneaky magic, too.

Preparation: You will need one double face card, such as the four of diamonds on one side and the jack of spades on the other side. This card is placed into your outer handkerchief pocket of your coat, with the jack of spades facing out.

To perform: Fan your pack of cards and remove the four of diamonds and the jack of spades, stating that you wish two cards of contrasting colors. Display both cards and place them side by side face up on the table, the four of diamonds to the left of the jack of spades.

With the left hand turn the four of diamonds face down on the table. The right hand now picks up the jack of spades and places it into your handkerchief pocket, face

out. (This goes behind the double face card already
there.) Now ask the spectator which card is on the table?
When he says the four of diamonds, ask him which card
you placed into your pocket?

When he says jack of spades, remove the double face
card (jack of spades showing) being careful not to expose
the back of the card and drop it, jack of spades up, be-
side the face down card (4D). Now pick up the jack of spades
(double face card) by the inner right hand corner with the
right index and thumb and slide it under the face down four
of diamonds, which is held at its inner left hand corner
with the middle finger of the left hand pressed against the
table.

Now you apparently turn over the four of diamonds, but
actually you perform the " Mexican Turnover" (described in Expert Card Technique and elsewhere). The
illusion is perfect. It merely looks as if you had taken
the jack of spades and flipped over the four of diamonds.

What has actually happened is that the four of diamonds
is still face down, and the double face card has now been
reversed, so as to show the four of diamonds. Now the
right hand picks up the four of diamonds (double face)
and places it into your handkerchief pocket, being careful
not to expose the reverse side of the card. It is placed
behind the regular jack of spades already there.

Ask the spectator which card you placed into your pocket. When he says the four of diamonds, say the magic
words and remove the jack of spades from your pocket,
turn over the face down card and show the four of diamonds. The two cards have changed places right under
his very nose.

You may now repeat the effect only now the double face
card in your pocket will be reversed. This is, the four
of diamonds will be face out in your pocket. This means
you will start by placing the regular four of diamonds
into your pocket first.

Note: In " Hilliard's Card Magic", page 444, you will
find a very clever trick, " A Card Change" by U.F.
Grant. The above may be combined with this trick or
used as a separate quickie. I use both effects and make
a whole mixed up routine out of them.

- - - - -

THE TREE OF . . . .

Effect: The magician hands the spectator a pack of cards, requesting that he remove any 3 spot card. When given the card, the performer rolls it into a tube and fastens it with a rubber band. The spectator is asked which card has been used, and when the spectator replies " The three of clubs", the performer says, " That's right, the TREE of ...... and proceeds to produce a miniature tree from the card. The tree grows until he shouts " TIMBER " and the tree topples to the table.

Preparation: Secure a roll of adding machine tape. I use National, size 9x. Proceed to make the familiar fir tree which should measure about 2 1/8" x 3/4". Also needed are a couple of rubber bands, and a pack of cards (Poker size). The tree and rubber band are placed into the left trouser pocket , ready

To Perform: Hand the spectator a pack of cards and ask him to remove any three spot card. When he removes it, take it from him (by force if necessary) and fashion a tube out of it by rolling the card on the table, from top to the bottom.

Then reach into the left pants pocket and remove the two rubber bands. Take one rubber band and fasten the card so it will not unroll, and hold in right hand. The left hand returns the remaining rubber band to the left pants pocket, stealing tree out of pocket.

Now transfer the card tube to the left hand, loading in the tree. By pressing the card with the thumb and fingers of the left hand, the load will stay within the card as the right hand pulls up tree.

Ask spectator which card you have, and when he says " the three of clubs" say: " That's right, the TREE" and produce the tree.

Keep pulling up tree until it is fully drawn up, and then shout " TIMBER" and bend tree so that it falls onto the table. This is not a great mystery but it's always good for a laff, so try it already.

- - - - -

IT CAN'T BE · · · · · · ·

Here is a real miracle type routine. It consists of
three phases, which may be performed independently.

Phase 1.
Effect: The performer removes a pack of cards from
the case and removes the four aces (Oh... not again!)
He then places them on the face of the pack and requests
spectator (I hope you have one available) to merely
think of one of the aces.

Stating that the Ace of Spades is too obvious, the performer places the Ace of Spades in his pocket, leaving
the three remaining aces to choose. Then the three
aces are turned face down and dealt onto the table or
bar. The rest of the pack, still face up, is then placed
to the side, right or left. Now for the climax (aren't
you glad?)

The performer asks the spectator (I hope he's still
there) which ace he thought of, and immediately the
performer removes the ace "thought of "from his
pocket. Performer explains that he wasn't quite sure
which ace the spectator would think of, so he took no
chances and then removes the remaining three aces
from his pocket.

The three cards face down on the table are then turned
up to reveal three indifferent cards. (I would probably
be indifferent, too, if I had to lie face down on a table
for that length of time.)

Method: (I had a hunch you'd ask). Yep, it's our old
friends, the double face cards (sneaky, huh?) First
remove from your trusty pack the regular four aces.
Take the ace of diamonds, the ace of clubs, and the
ace of hearts, in that order, and place them face out
in your right pants pocket. The ace of diamonds is
facing to the outside.

Place the three double face aces in any order in the
pack and lastly place the ace of spades (regular) near-
est the bottom face card. (Huh?) Replace the pack in
your case and you are ready to spring your trap. This
must be accomplished by cornering a spectator or two.

When this is accomplished you announce that you are
about to perform a card trick. I am not sure how they
will react, but go ahead anyway.

To perform: Remove the pack from the case and hold
it face up in the left hand. Spreading the cards, locate
the first ace, which will be the ace of spades, and out-
jog it. Then do the same thing with the three remaining aces. With the right hand remove the four protruding aces and place them face up on the pack, which is
held face up in the left hand.

Now spread the four aces and at the same time secure a
break of three cards below the aces. Square the seven
cards, and then just spread the four aces, still holding
the break of seven cards. Ask the spectator to merely
think of one of the aces, but not to think of the ace of
spades, as it is too obvious.

To prevent this situation, the performer (this should
by now be you) places the ace of spades in his pocket.
To do this, place the ace of spades facing out behind the
three aces already there. Now the performer turns the
three remaining aces face down. Actually you turn the
six cards face down and immediately deal the three face
down cards on the table.

Naturally the double face cards are now turned over, so
as to appear as indifferent cards (that word again).
Place the pack aside and ask the spectator which ace
he thought of. Look surprised and remove his ace from
your pocket, which you can do as you have the aces in
order in your pocket.

Pause (so that the effect will refresh so to speak) and
then explain that you had no way of knowing which ace
he would think of, so you thought it best to have all four
aces in your pocket. Here you remove the three remaining aces from your pocket. Turn over the three face
down cards on the table, which will be three indifferent
cards, and place these on the bottom of the face up pack,
which had been placed aside.

Display the four aces and place them face up, with the
ace of spades at the face to one side (the four cards
squared). You are now ready for phase 2.

Phase 2.
Effect: Twelve indifferent cards are counted off the
major portion of the pack and are held face up in the
left hand. The four aces are then added to the cards
in the left hand. Then the four aces are dealt face up
on the table in a row and three cards are dealt face down
on each ace. Since the ace of spades was the trouble-
maker in the first part of the trick, it is removed, along
with the three face down cards, and the spectator is
asked to sit on the four cards.

Remaining on the table are three face up aces with three
face down cards on each. The performer then gathers
up the nine face down cards and turns them face up. Then
the three aces are added to the nine cards and turned
face down and dealt on to the table. The remaining nine
cards are then dealt face up on to the table.

Now the performer rubs each face down ace(?) and then
slowly turns over each card, showing that the three aces
have disappeared. The spectator is then asked to remove the four cards he has been sitting on, and the four
aces appear, as if by magic.

Preparation: none, as at the completion of Phase 1,you
are all set to go into this Phase.

Method: First gather the four aces in a packet (ace of
spades on the face) and turn face down on the table. Then
pick up the pack and hold face up in the left hand. (The
first three cards on the face of the deck are the double
face cards). Begin counting the cards into the right hand.

Take the first card and counting, "one", place the second card under the first, saying, "two ". The third
card is placed under the second card and is injogged
slightly. Continue counting cards under those held in
the right hand until you have twelve cards.

Then the left hand places the remainder of the pack,
still face up, off to one side. The cards in the right
hand are now transferred to the left hand, where they
are held face up with the third card still injogged. At
this point, no attempt is made to square up the packet.

The right hand now picks up the four face down aces and
deposits the four cards face down on the packet held in

14

the left hand. Now the packet is squared, at the same time getting a break under the seventh card, due to the injogged card.

The seven cards are turned face up on the packet. The situation is now this: The first three cards will be double face aces, followed by the ace of spades, then by the three regular aces, then by 9 indifferent cards. Hold the packet so that you can push off one card at a time and deal the first double face ace on to the table.

Be careful so as not to flash the underneath side when dealing the double face cards. Then deal the second double face ace to the right of the first. Do the same with the third ace, placing it to the right of the two aces. The regular ace of spades will now appear on the face of the packet held in the left hand.

Naturally you cannot deal the ace of spades as you would expose the regular aces underneath. So turn your left hand back up and with the left forefinger on the left ace and the first finger and third finger of the right hand on the other two aces proceed to move the three cards to the right about four inches to make room on the left side for the ace of spades, which you draw out from the bottom of the packet with the right hand and turn it face up and place it to the left of the three tabled aces.

The left hand now drops the packet it has been holding face down onto the table. Now both hands arrange the four aces on the table so that they're in a neat row. This gives you an excuse to pick up the packet of twelve cards now face down in the left hand as for dealing.

The three regular aces are now on the bottom of the packet and on the table from left to right are the regular ace of spades, and then the three double face aces. Now state that you will deal three cards onto each ace. Start to the right and deal three cards onto each ace, working to the left.

This will bring the last three cards (the regular aces) onto the ace of spades, all the cards being dealt face down onto the face up aces. Proceed to explain that since the ace of spades caused confusion in the first trick, you shall remove it.

15

Pick up the ace of spades packet and ask spectator if he will sit on the packet, so that no one can come in contact with the four cards. Now gather up the nine face down cards and turn them face up in the left hand and spread them to show, at the same time injogging the third card a little.

Square up the packet securing the break at the third card and with the right hand pick up the aces on the table and drop them face up on to the packet held in the left hand.

Now apparently turn the three aces face down, actually turning the cards from the break which will be six cards. This gives you three indifferent cards face down and reverses the double face aces, so as to show indifferent cards.

Deal the three face down cards onto the table, calling them aces and immediately spread out the nine cards left face up, showing no aces and drop this packet on to the remainder of the deck which is face up off to the side.

The three face down aces (?) are now turned face up to show that the aces have disappeared and ask spectator to remove the cards he has been sitting on all the while. Much to his surprise he finds the four aces. While the spectator is removing the cards place the three indifferent cards into the center of the pack. You are now ready to enter Phase 3.

Phase 3.
Effect: Once again the four aces are shown and dealt on to the table. The ace packet is placed into the magician's outer breast pocket and the indifferent packet is placed into the spectator's outer breast pocket. The magician takes the troublesome ace of spades from his pocket and places it into the spectator's pocket, at the same time removing an indifferent card from the packet in the spectator's pocket.

The magic words are spoken and once again it is found that the spectator now holds the four aces and the magician has the four indifferent cards. This now completes the three phases and at the same time gets rid of the gimmicks in a natural way, leaving you as clean as can be.

Preparation: none, as at the completion of phase two you are ready for phase three.

Method: At the completion of phase 2 you will find yourself with the three double face cards (indifferent cards showing) on the face up pack held in the left hand. The four (regular) aces are on the table face up. Turn the pack in the left hand face down, being careful to keep the pack square, so the double face cards will not show at the bottom of the deck.

Now pick up the ace of spades and place it face up on the face down deck. Follow the same procedure with the other three aces, one at a time. Spread out the four aces, and while displaying them face up on the face down deck, the next four cards on the top of the deck are secretly gotten together under the aces as they are squared up to the pack, and removed by the right hand with the right thumb at the inner right corner, and the second finger holding them at the outer right hand corner.

The aces are then turned, one at a time face down on top of the deck. To do this, the left thumb pulls the ace to the left of the packet held in the right hand. Then the ace is levered face down on to the deck with the packet held in the right hand.

The first three aces are flipped over in this manner on to the deck and the fourth ace (spades) together with the four cards concealed underneath are momentarily deposited on top of the deck, before turning the ace of spades face down on to the pack.

This maneuver places the four indifferent cards second third, fourth and fifth followed by the three aces. This above series of moves is known as Marlo's Secret Card Add, and may be found in the Ireland publication HANDBOOK OF CARD SLEIGHTS by Al Leech, page 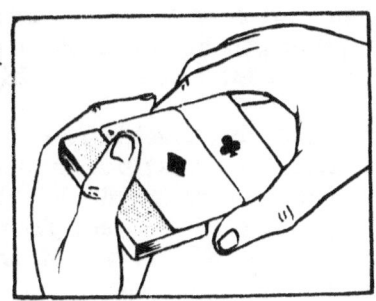 22. The illustration shows the action of turning the aces on to the deck.

Now deal the top card, the ace of spades, face up on to the table, and deal the next three cards, apparently the aces, face down on top of the ace of spades. Now to the right of these four cards, deal the next card (it will be an indifferent card) face up on the table,and then deal the next three cards (in reality the three aces) face down in a row onto the face up indifferent card.

Next turn the deck in the left hand face up and place in the left hand coat pocket, the deck facing the body. The reason for this will be clear later. Now pick up the ace of spades and turn it face down. Holding the ace of spades in the right hand, scoop up the three aces with it and square the packet, showing the ace of spades at the face.

Actually you have three indifferent cards and the ace of spades. You then place the packet into your outer breast pocket with the ace of spades facing the body. Then pick up the face up indifferent card, turn it face down and scoop up the three face down cards (three aces).

Square and turn packet face up showing the indifferent card at the face of the packet and place into spectator's outer breast pocket, the indifferent card facing his body. Now reach into your pocket with your right hand and remove the ace of spades and place on the table. Reach into the spectator's pocket and remove the indifferent card and place on table.

Have spectator place the ace of spades into his pocket, while you are placing the indifferent card into your pocket. Announce that the ace of spades is again a trouble-maker and remove the four cards from your pocket and show them to be indifferent cards. Have spectator remove the four cards from his pocket.

Once again he has the four aces. You now reach into your left hand coat pocket and thumb off the three cards from the face of the deck (these are the double face cards) and remove deck from the pocket. You are now clean, finished, and out of breath, I hope.

This may read very long and complicated but if you will take the cards and follow it thru a couple of times, I am sure you will be pleased with the results. Naturally any one of the phases may be done independently, but the whole routine will make them see real magic.

- - - - - - -

A PRETTY SNEAKY NUDIST..........ROUTINE

Here is one of my pet routines. It's wonderful for that
occasion when someone says: " Do us a trick". This
has never happened to me, but I always carry it, just
in case.

Effect: Performer explains that he would like to do a
card trick but he can't and proceeds to explain why.

Preparation: Secure a pack of Hull's Nudist Deck from
your magic dealer. This is a standard item. If you are
not familiar with the deck, read the instructions that
come with it and then you will be ready for this routine.

Place the deck into your pocket and wait for someone
to ask you to do a trick. This may take some time.

Note: In handling the deck, the cards are held face up,
that is, with the faces up, even tho you cannot see them.
This will be the position of the deck, unless otherwise
stated.

To perform: " Gee, I would like to do a card trick for
you, but I can't." (remove the deck from your pocket).
"I hate excuses but you see they are a little behind in
production this year." (Remove cards from their case
and show them to be blank on both sides. Do this by
running the cards from hand to hand on both sides.)

"And to think they had them sticking out their ears last
year." (The pack is now squared and held in the left
hand as for dealing, the cards being face up, as stated
above). " But I can tell you about the card trick I usually
do. It will be almost as boring. First, of course, I
always shuffle the cards. Union."

(Here shuffle the cards in overhand style with the cards
being shuffled from the face up position. This way they
will not separate during the shuffle).

"Notice how I shuffle? Used to be a chicken plucker."
(If you get a laugh here, turn to person and say: "You
too?") (At the finish of the shuffle return cards squared

up into left hand as for dealing. Now spread the cards as if you wanted one taken, saying: "First I usually have a card taken" and before spectator can take one pull back the pack and square it, turn it over and spread and say: "I don't even remember which side but it wouldn't make any difference anyway."

Here square pack and turn over again. This will bring the pack face up again in the left hand. "Let's assume you had taken a card. You must look at it, remember it, and return it to the pack. And my job would be to find it. Now let's say you had taken the " (here you give the pack a cut, cutting the cards using the right thumb at the rear of the pack and the second and third finger of the right hand to cut off a portion of the pack.)

(Place this cut off section under the portion of the pack left in the left hand. This will bring a card to the face of the deck and a back to the bottom of the pack, which should not be exposed as yet.)

Immediately as you cut the cards and see the face of the card, say: "Four of spades, " thereby finishing the sentence started above, just before the cut.

"Of course,"you continue , "the four of spades is very easy to find, as it is the only card in the deck." (Here you spread the cards from hand to hand showing all blanks, except the four of spades).

"I hate to do it the hard way." (The pack is now held squared in the left hand). "Unfortunately there is one trouble. Cards should have a design on the back." (Here turn over the four of spades showing it to be blank on the back and flip it back to the four of spades side on to the pack.)

"And you can see a person could go snow blind looking at these so I have worked out a system. I hold the pack in the right hand"(the right thumb at the rear and the fingers of the right hand lift the squared pack out of the left hand) "and tap it against the tip of my left forefinger."

(The left hand is curled into a fist with the forefinger extending straight up from the table and the pack in the right hand is tapped against the finger so that the bottom of the pack strikes the nail of the finger.)

"This does two things. First, it breaks your finger nail, if you hit it too hard. And second, it gives you a nice red back." (Here the pack is turned over exposing the card with the back on it, and immediately the pack is turned again face up into the left hand.)

"Which of course matches the face. Now actually this isn't as confusing as it should be. It would really be confusing if we had other cards, like the ace of clubs, the jack of hearts, and the ten of clubs."

(The right hand lifts off a group of cards from the deck in the left hand exposing a card. This is done three times, each time replacing the cut off section, only to lift another portion, exposing, for example, the above three cards. At the completion of the cuts the pack is squared up in the left hand and immediately the cards are spread from hand to hand, showing all blanks, and you say:)

"But unfortunately we do not have these cards. It would be nice. It would be nice, too, if the four of spades(top card) had a design on the back." (The four of spades is turned over, blank back shown, and then turned back to the face). " Will you touch the card right in the center? "

(The pack is held out to the spectator so that he can touch the card with his finger. As he touches the card in the center the right hand picks up the top card (four of spades). Actually a double lift is executed, but it will be automatic due to the construction of the pack.)

(The card is shown on both sides, displaying the four of spades to now have a back design. The two cards are returned to the pack and the four of spades (single card) is turned over as you say:)

" Before you touched the card it didn't have a back." (This will now let them see that the four of spades once again does not have a back design. Square pack and hold face up in left hand. Once again extend pack to spectator and ask:)

" Will you touch all four of your fingers on the face of the pack," (He does). " Now wiggle them up and down". (He does). " You know why I asked you to do that? Because that makes you the Liberace of the playing cards

21

and I've never seen one. Now by your wiggling your
fingers we have all the cards."

(The pack is taken by the right hand and riffled to show
all the cards, faces and backs - as per instructions in
the Nudist Deck - . Do this twice so that they see lots
of cards and then quickly square up pack face up into
left hand and immediately spread cards from hand to
hand showing all blanks, except the top card, as you
say:)

"Before you wiggled your fingers we didn't have the
other cards." (Pause slightly for a reaction and then
say:)" And that's the reason I can't do the card trick"
(here the bottom card is shifted from the bottom to the
top of the pack over the top card, the four of spades,
a la color change) " I had in mind. But if I had the
cards" (here the cards are spread from hand to hand,
squared, turned over, and again spread from hand to
hand showing blank cards on both sides), "I would be
happy to do the trick for you."

"Maybe next time I see you, I'll have the cards and
then I'll do the trick for you." (Cards are now placed
into case and put into pocket as you mumble:)

" A person can't work without the proper tools. They
just don't make 'em like they used to, I guess." (Finish).

Note: This presentation eliminates the spectator reach-
ing for the deck to examine after the trick. You have
joked the deck right into your pocket with a good excuse.
Give this a try and I hope you have as many laffs as I
have had with this routine.

- - - - - -

CHRISTINE (?), THE SNEAKY DUCK

Here is a routine with the mechanical duck Jo-Ann,
(Card Pickin, that is), using alphabet cards. You will
find this most valuable for that special occasion such
as birthdays, anniversaries, and business associations
(if any).

Preparation: Secure a duck, (Hamilton make called
Jo-Ann) and proceed to drill a small hole in the tail

FIG. 1

FIG. 2

FIG. 3

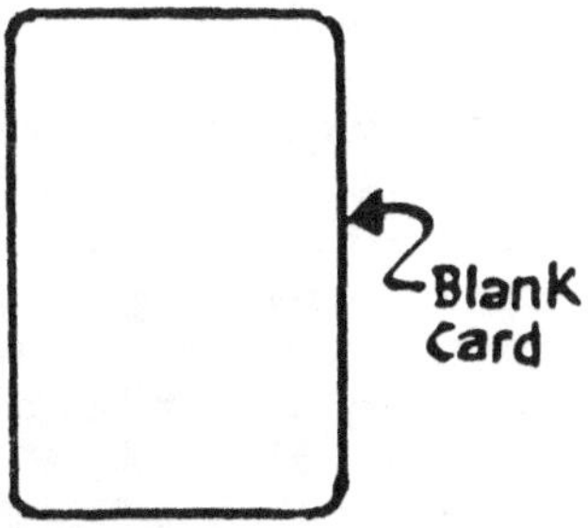

FIG. 4

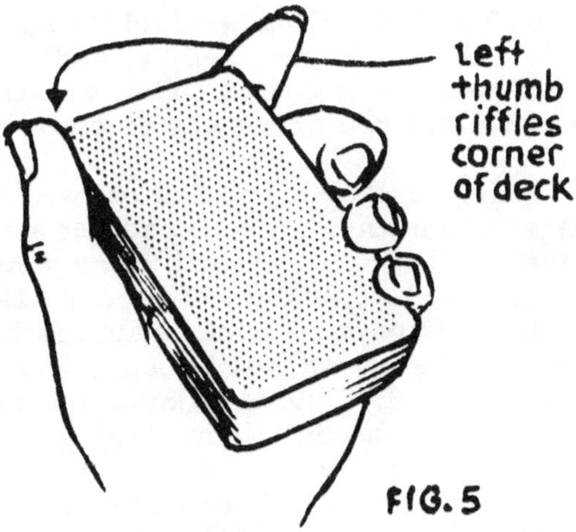

Blank card

Left thumb riffles corner of deck

FIG. 5

about a half an inch deep. From a woman's hat trim counter buy a goofy, bushy feather and place in hole for tail. This makes it removable for packing. Go to a doll supply house and get a little bonnet and fix onto the duck's head. Mine is held on by a short length of elastic. Duck should now look like figure 1.

Place a twelve inch varicolor silk into recess in bottom of deck. Obtain a deck of Alphabet cards (you should buy two, so as to have enough letters to spell anything). Also you will need a blank face card to match deck, a three and a half of clubs card to match deck and another blank face card, with all the letters of the alphabet inked on the face as in figure 2.

The corners of the letter "Y" card are trimmed as in figure 3. Also trim the corners of the blank card as in figure 4.

The deck is set up as follows: take the blank card and place face up on the table. Take the three and a half of clubs (the trick called Miko gives you half a dozen of these - any magic shop has them) and place face up on the blank card, followed by the " mixed up " card, followed by the "Y" card. These three cards are followed by cards P, P, A, H , Y, A, D, H, T, R, I, B. (This will spell out Happy Birthday backwards. This is advisable so that the complete message is not given away too soon.)

Now the remainder of the alphabet deck is cut into two face up packets and the above stack is sandwiched between these two packets of cards. The pack is now placed into a case and you are ready to come forth.

To perform: Bring forth Duck and cards and say:"I'd like you to meet Christine." (You may get a little giggle here, but pause and say:) "Her last name would have been Jorgensen, but she Ducked in time.... Now Christine does a sneaky little card trick, which is quite unusual, as a recent survey shows, because Ducks do not play cards. It seems that ducks enjoy doing many thing. but card tricks are not among them.

" So since Christine cannot tell the difference between the ace of clubs and the jack of diamonds -- not that she has anything against them -- I had a special deck of cards made for her." (Remove deck from pocket, remove cards, turning them face up and spread a few of the bottom cards, saying:)

" These are alphabet cards, the letter A, the letter X, the letter D, which is one of the reasons I enjoy working with Christine. In the few short months we 've been to-gether I've already memorized thirteen of these things. Now to show how sneaky Christine is, I would like to have a card selected."

(The pack is turned face down and held in the left hand, so that the left thumb can riffle down the outer left cor-ner , figure 5. Ask a spectator to say " stop "as you riffle the pack. Time his " stop " so that you stop on the corner short. Now by lifting the packet above the break, obtained by the corner short, you show the bot-tom card of this packet , which will be the letter "Y".)

(The above force is my time riffle force, explained in "Close Up Time". We still have a few copies left (sneaky plug!)

After a number of spectators have seen the bottom card of the packet held now in the right hand, the packet is dropped onto the remainder of the deck held in the left hand. Carefully square pack and explain that Christine will now attempt to find the card. To help her a little you will give the deck a cut to mix her up. (Huh.)

Due to your set up, by holding the deck face down in your left hand as for dealing, the right thumb riffles up the inner left corner until you reach the corner short. This will be the blank card. The pack is immediately cut at this point. By completing the cut you now have your complete set up on top of the deck.

The cards are now placed into the "feed box" and you state that Christine will find the card. Explain that Christine will do this under a handicap. Here remove the 12 inch silk from Christine 's recess and display the vari-colored silk.

"Many people do not realize what this really is. It really is a collector 's item. This is an authentic Babushka from a shrunken head. Very rare." (As you say this, spin the silk and proceed to blindfold the duck. Get

25

duck into position for operating mechanism and say:
"Christine, are you ready?" Have duck nod. Then
say: "Remember, Christine, I will only ask the question once, and your answer will have to be accepted."
Duck nods again.

"Now, Christine, what is the gentleman's letter?"
Pause and then have duck bring up blank card.

"I'm sorry, Christine, you have just missed the 64,000
grain question." (Topical at this writing). "But we will
give you another chance, won't we?" (Turn to audience).

"If you get the correct card this time we will award
you with a white on white duck's egg, all right?" (Duck
nods). "Now what was the gentleman's letter?" (Duck
brings up three and a half of clubs card.) "Well, at
least it goes to show you she's not a sore loser. She
apparently is a little mixed up at this point."

(Duck brings up mixed up alphabet card). "Maybe if we
could have a little prompting from the audience....sir,
what was your letter?" (When he answers "Y" say:)
"Well, we don't want her to go home disappointed. Now
what was your letter?" (Again he says "Y").

Turn to someone else and say: "Did you see the letter?"
When they answer "Y", say: "You're no more help than
he is...." (Don't drag out this Abbott and Costello bit
too much. Say:) "Oh, maybe you mean the letter Y."
When they agree, have duck bring up letter Y. After
applause, place the Y card to your left on the table. All
previous cards are of course piled off to one side.

State that Chrstine has a chance for a consolation prize.
"To win the prize she must do this". Duck now reaches
down into feed box and pulls up cards , which are placed
facing the spectators next to the Y card, working to your
right, upside down, until the message HAPPY BIRTH-
DAY is spelled out, or whatever message the occasion
calls for.

Wait for your applause - you can't miss. Then say:
"Christine, for answering the question correctly, we
have arranged to have you shipped, by non-scheduled
bus line to New York, where you are to be tarred and
feathered on the Ed Sullivan Show."

You may now put the duck away and take your bow, and don't forget to duck. Naturally, if you were doing a show for the Ford Motor Company, you would spell out FORD for the finish. I mention this as it is very commercial and it's helped keep us off the street for some time now.

Here are a few extra things to throw into the routine: "I bet when you first saw Christine, you thought someone had said the secret word." Put a small coon skin cap on duck and call him Davey Duckett.

- - - - - -

FLAMING HAN PING CHIEN(Presentation)

Those of you familiar with the standard Han Ping Chien Coin Trick will appreciate this novel presentation. Since all I have added to the effect is a kitchen match, I will refer you to Bobo's excellent COIN MAGIC, pages 190-193 for the handling. You will note that my effect requires only four coins. This is, I believe, less confusing, more direct and entertaining. Naturally, you may use the traditional eight coins if you wish. (Flaunt your wealth - see if I care.)

Effect: Four half dollars are displayed on the table, along with one kitchen type match. Two half dollars are openly placed into your left hand and the remaining two half dollars and the kitchen match are picked up with the right hand.

Now slowly close each hand into a fist and explain that you intend to pass the coins thru the table. Your right hand now goes underneath table, apparently to tap under side of table to show solid. (Here the right hand deposits the two half dollars on your right knee, and immediately taps bottom of table top.)

The right hand is now brought out from under table as you show two half dollars in your left hand, slapping coins on to table. They are then picked up again by left hand and the right hand slaps the match on table, at same time releasing coins from left hand as in standard effect. The right hand now picks up the two coins and the kitchen match, and once again returns under table.

27

(As soon as your right hand is under table, pick up the
two coins from your knee and move your hand to the
center of the table). Your left hand (now empty) is held
over the center of the table from above. Suddenly there
is a crackling (your right hand strikes match on bottom
of table) and the left hand is quickly opened. The half
dollars have disappeared.

The right hand is then brought slowly from under the
table, where the match is seen burning, held by the
right thumb and forefinger, the remaining three fingers
closed into a fist (holding coins).

As the right hand is brought over the table, the match
still burning, the bottom three fingers open and the
four half dollars spill on the table.

You now hold the match off to your right and blow
down your left sleeve (familiar move) and the match
goes out. (Note, the match is held in just the right
position for the above move.) The striking and burning of the match are very effective. Give it a try.

- - - - - - - - -

A LAS VEGAS FAIRY TALE

One of my favorite coin routines is the Cap and the
Pence, or more popularly known as the Stack of Quarters. In an effort to work out something a little different, I added the dice and the Las Vegas theme. This
change makes the effect more logical and is quite
amusing to the spectators.

Effect: The sneaky magician removes a small purse
from his pocket and a small leather cone. Opening the
purse, the magician removes a small die and six quarters. The spectator is requested to place the coins in
the magician's hand, counting them aloud.

The spectator is then asked to examine the leather cone
and when he is satisfied as to its innocence, the magician requests the spectator to hold out his right hand,
palm down, and about ten inches off the table. The magician then places the six quarters on the back of the
spectator's hand and then places the small die on top
of the six quarters.

28

The magician then covers the quarters and die with the leather cone. He pushes down on top of the cone with his right forefinger and the six quarters are seen to penetrate the spectator's hand, falling to the table. A moment later the cone is lifted, and all that is left is the small die, proving that the quarters actually penetrated the spectator's hand.

Preparation: Secure a small purse, found in novelty stores. Mine came on a key chain, just big enough to hold six quarters. See illustration.

Small Purse

FIG. 6

Also you will need the quarter stack (6 coins high) and 6 regular quarters. A leather cone to fit loosely over the six quarters and a wooden or cardboard cone for the leather one to fit over. This keeps the cone in shape when carried in your pocket. My inner cone is cardboard and was made from a string cone, used to wind string around.

Now obtain two small dice. These should measure 5/16 " and may be found in novelty shops. White ones are best. Fix a small daub of wax to one die on the one spot side, and place into purse with the 6 regular quarters. Place the other die into the recess of the fake stack of quarters and place it into your right coat pocket, along with the tiny purse.

Place the cone(s) into your outer breast pocket of your coat and you are ready to perform. If you wish, a small flat rubber band may be put on the stack, to keep the small die from dropping out, but I have never found this necessary. If the die becomes separated from the stack it takes just a second to replace.

To perform: Announce that you have just returned from Las Vegas and you'd like to tell them a little fairy tale. Begin by removing cone(s) from your outer pocket and separate them, returning the inner cardboard cone to your pocket. Explain cone by saying: " One small fairy dunce cap, size 2 1/4, for sitting in small, small corners. "

Then reach into right coat pocket and finger palm stack with die, gripped by the last three fingers and the palm, with the opening against the palm. As this is done, immediately pick up small purse with the forefinger and thumb and bring out and display.

Place purse on table, saying: " This is all they allowed me to bring back. " Now pick up purse with empty left hand and open it with the right forefinger and thumb, keeping stack concealed by the closed fingers of the right hand. Remove small die and place on table with the two spot uppermost, the six spot facing spectators. This will bring the wax toward you.

As you remove die, say: " And this is the cause of it all. " Now dump out the six quarters from the purse on to the table with the left hand and close purse with the right forefinger and thumb, and quickly return purse into right coat pocket with right hand (naturally).

As the coins are dumped on the table, say: " This is the REMAINS. I'm loaded. " Now request spectator to count the coins into your left palm, which you hold out to him, saying: " This even looks like Las Vegas. "

Ask spectator to count the coins aloud, and as the last coin is counted, the hand is shaken, cupping hand slightly to bring all the coins together into a stack, at the base of the two middle fingers (finger palm position).

Now point to cone on table and request spectator to examine same, saying: " Will you please see if the owner's initials are on the sweatband, and at the same time make sure the hat is empty. " As the spectator picks up the cone to examine, the two hands come together and the coins are apparently picked up by the right forefinger and thumb, and then transferred back to the left forefinger and thumb, the forefinger on the face of the stack and the thumb on the back, holding the die in place, and covering same from prying eyes.

Actually, you have switched the stack for the real coins. The real coins are finger palmed in the left hand, at the base of the two middle fingers and the stack is be-

ing held by the forefinger and thumb, as just explained.
The actual mechanics for the switch are as follows.

As the right hand moves toward the left hand to take
the coins from it, the fake stack is brought near the tips
of the two middle fingers. This is done by merely opening the fingers of the right hand slightly, the hand being back up and slightly tipped downward. This is done
as the hand moves toward the left hand.

As the hands come together, place the right thumb on
the bottom of the stack (the ball of the thumb rests on
the nested die) lying on the curled fingers of the palm
down right hand, and slide the fake stack forward and
place it directly above the real quarters in the left hand.
The curled fingers conceal this action.

The left hand retains the real quarters finger palmed,
while the fake stack is brought into view by the right
hand, which grips it between the tips of the right forefinger and thumb.

The left hand now turns palm inward and the stack is
transferred to the left forefinger and thumb, as previously described.

PLEASE do not make a magical MOVE when doing the
switch. Just bring both hands together, pick up the
quarters (?) and don't hurry. There will be very little
attention on you at this moment, as the spectator will
be absorbed with the cone.

By this time the cone will have been examined. Ask
spectator to hold out his right hand, palm downward.
Demonstrate with your right hand. As he holds out his
hand, take the stack back with the right forefinger and
thumb and under the pretext of steadying his hand, grasp
it by the little finger side with your left hand in such a
manner that your thumb will lie on the back of his hand
and your fingers curled underneath - curled just enough
so that he cannot feel the finger palmed quarters.

Now place the fake stack on the back of his right hand
being careful not to let die be seen, when placing stack
down. Even up the stack and pick up die from table and
give it a quarter turn toward you, as you place it on top
of quarter stack. (This will place waxed side against

stack). Give it a little downward pressure as you do this. Thus it will now be stuck to the stack.

Now say that you will give a real Las Vegas demonstration. Pick up cone with right hand and place over the stack and die on spectator's hand. Then lift cone once so that spectator can see quarters and die, and then re-cover.

As spectator is asked to say: " Las Vegas,"you put the tip of your right forefinger on top of the cone and push lightly downward. As spectator says: " Las Vegas", release coins from left hand saying: " That's the way it is in Las Vegas. Money slips right thru your hand."

Pause a moment for the effect to sink in and then grasp cone at the base with right forefinger and thumb and lift up cone together with stack by applying a little pressure, saying: " All that's left is my little souvenir." And die is exposed.

As spectator's eyes are on die, loosen your grip on cone, and allow the stack with the die fastened to it to drop into the cupped fingers, and toss cone on the table. Immediately reach into right coat pocket, dropping stack and die and pick up small purse and bring out. Slowly place quarters and die into purse and replace into coat pocket, as you say: " And that's a true Las Vegas Fairy Tale".

Spectators will want to examine cone, so leave on table a few moments before putting away.

Note: For a little different finish, load into the stack a red die of the same size as the white one, and when cone is lifted, you will have a color change. Say: " It's easy to change color in Las Vegas - only it's usually from red to white."

- - - - -

SNEAKY HALF DOLLAR IN BOTTLE

This is one of my pet close up routines. I've kept this presentation to myself for a number of years, and so there you are ...

Preparation: You will need one folding half dollar and a regular half to match. One Anti-Gravico bottle gimmick, a wooden hook (made from a small paint brush handle, as shown in figure 7. Also a tiny wooden figure, the size of a match (made from a match, figures, huh?) See figure 8. On the table or bar you will need

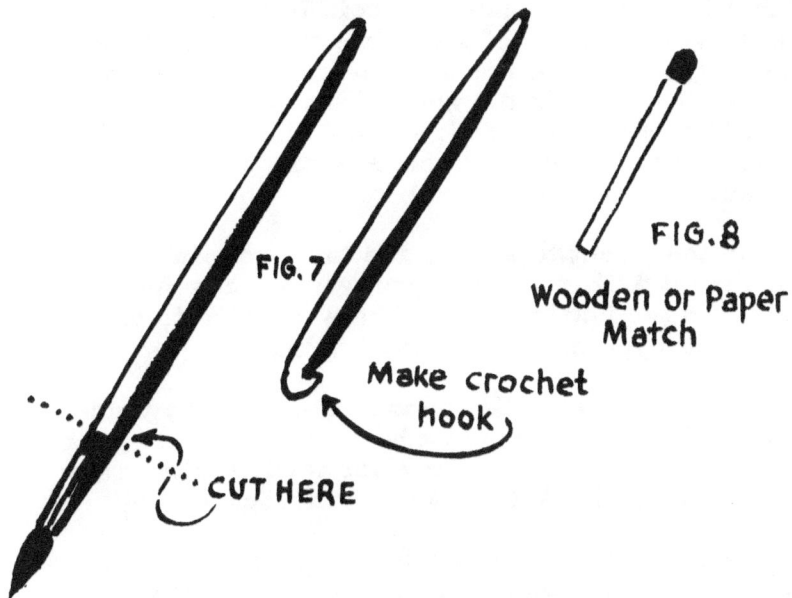

FIG. 7

FIG. 8

Wooden or Paper Match

Make crochet hook

CUT HERE

a coke bottle (or Pepsi bottle.... there will be no favorites shown in my book!) and a glass of water (huh?)

Place the regular half dollar into the right coat pocket, along with the Anti-Gravico gimmick. Also have a pocket handkerchief in this pocket. Into your left coat pocket place the folding half and the small match size wooden figure. (This may be just a paper match with a simple sketch of a figure drawn on in ink). Into your outer breast pocket place the wooden hook. You are now ready....

To Perform: State that you saw a magician do a wonderful trick the other day. Say: " He filled up a bottle with water". (Fill half way up). "And then he removed from his pocket a half dollar."

(Here both hands go into their respective coat pockets in search of a half dollar. The right hand finger palms the Anti-Gravico gimmick and comes out apparently

empty, while the left hand removes the folding half
and slaps it on to the table. (Do this boldly). Now
sweep the half dollar off the table with the left hand,
and under cover of this movement, get the coin folded
for insertion into the bottle.

State that the magician held the coin in his fist and
placed it over the neck of the bottle. (Do this). "Then
with his right hand, he pounded the coin into the bottle."
(As the left hand holds the neck of the bottle, insert the
coin into the neck and the right hand closes into a fist,
hiding gimmick palmed, and strikes top of the left fist,
which causes coin to pop into bottle.

Pause for the effect to set in, and then explain that the
part of the trick that amazed you was not how he got
the coin into the bottle, but how he was going to get it
out? Say that you have tried everything.

You even turned the bottle upside down, but the coin
wouldn't drop out. (Here you have grasped the top of
the bottle to invert it with the right hand, at the same
time slipping on the Anti-Gravico gimmick.)

The bottle is now held upside down with the left hand
on the bottom of the bottle, as you say: "I thought it
would maybe drop out." (All of a sudden it will hit
them that the water is not coming out.)

State that you've tried everything. You even had a
hook made to pull the coin out. (Here remove hook
from pocket and insert up into bottle, as if trying to
hook coin.) Remove wooden hook and place back into
pocket.

Say you even hired a midget. Transfer bottle to your
right hand and remove small figure and proceed to
float it up into bottle, explaining that you thought maybe
he could push coin out. But this didn't work, either.

Finally say: " This magician finally told me his secret.
The only way to get the coin out is to pour out the water."
(Here grasp top of bottle with the right hand and turn
bottle right side up, at the same time stealing off the
gimmick with the right hand.

The left hand now slowly pours all the water back into the glass, the little match figure going into the glass. The bottle, now empty of water, is again turned upside down and held by the left hand.)

Explain that to get the coin out of the bottle, the bottle must be dry. Reach into your right coat pocket and remove handkerchief and dry off bottle. Then return handkerchief to pocket and drop anti-Gravico gimmick, at the same time palming out regular half dollar. Both moves are done at the same time.

The right hand with the regular half dollar finger palmed grasps the middle of the bottle as the left hand comes down to circle the neck and mouth of the bottle in such a way as to be sure to catch the folding half when it pops out of the bottle. Thus gripped, by shaking the bottle downward, the folding half will come into the left hand.

As soon as this happens, immediately remove the left hand with folding half and continue to shake the bottle with the right hand. Let the regular half dollar, held against the outside of the bottle by the right hand, rattle against the bottle and it will appear for a moment as tho the coin is still in the bottle.

Then on a final hard shake, release coin on the downward motion and it will look like the coin came out of the bottle. As they are examining the coin and bottle, go south with the folding half (if you will excuse the expression.)

Note: You are two moves ahead of them from the start. Try this and watch their faces as you turn bottle upside down. The props are easy to make or get, and well worth the little trouble.

- - - - - - -

CUT DOWN TO HALF A PACK

The performer holds a pack of cigarettes in his hand and asks if the audience has read any of the articles on smoking? When the spectators reply, the magician says he's read all the articles and they all suggest a person should cut down. So he has solved the whole thing by cutting down to a "Half a Pack a Day." As he

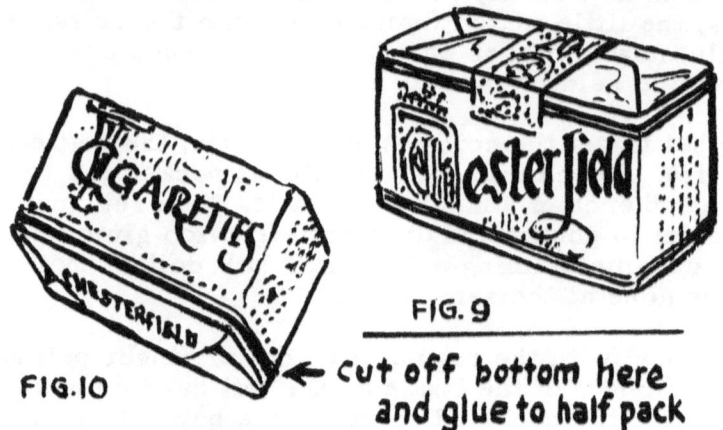

FIG. 9

FIG. 10 ← cut off bottom here and glue to half pack

Bottom of whole pack

says this, the pack is placed on the table, where it is seen to be just a half pack as in figure 9.

To make, get a pack of Chesterfields, as this is the best package due to the wording on the label. Take a razor blade and cut pack in half. Discard the half cigarettes in the bottom half and then trim the bottom of the package as shown in figure 10.

Now glue with rubber cement on to the top half and let dry. Now by holding the pack so that it sticks out of the top of the fist it will look like a regular pack, and this way the stunt is concealed until ready to lay the pack on the table.

- - - - - - -

CUT OUT THIS TONITE

FIG. 11

This is good to combine with the above gag. Mention that your doctor has made you cut out liquor, late hours, smoking .. in fact, you just cut out this tonite. Here you quickly open a little cardboard folder you've been holding and pull out a string of PAPER DOLLS. Refold into folder, fold up and steal away into the night. See figure 11 for appearance of folder and dolls.

- - - - - - -

BALL POINT PEN

The performer displays a ball point pen which looks normal, and asks if they have seen the new ball point pen? When they answer, suddenly a little red ball appears on the end of the pen, truly a ball point pen.

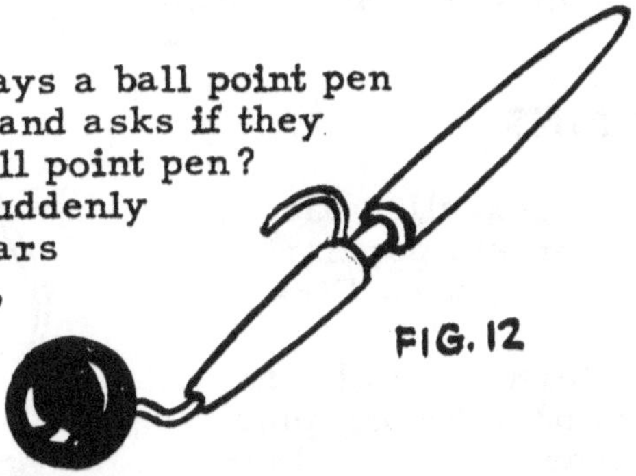

FIG. 12

Remark: "It's not much good as a pen, but it does help keep us up when writing under water."

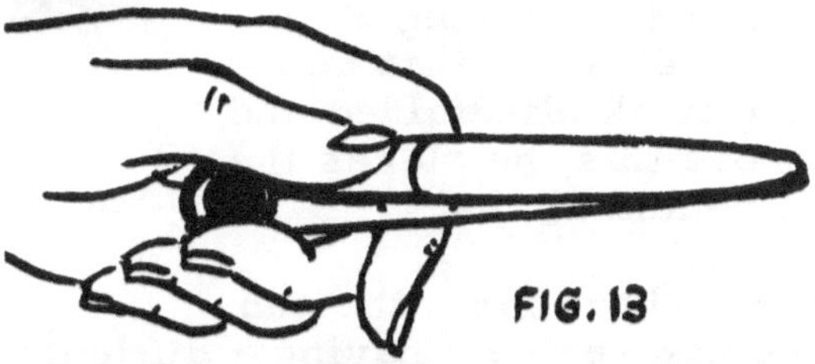

FIG. 13

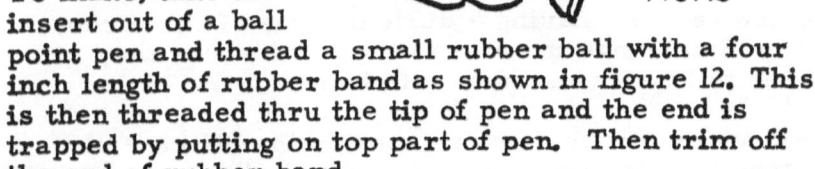

To make, take the insert out of a ball point pen and thread a small rubber ball with a four inch length of rubber band as shown in figure 12. This is then threaded thru the tip of pen and the end is trapped by putting on top part of pen. Then trim off the end of rubber band.

To perform, hold pen and ball as in figure 13 and suddenly release ball to point of pen.

- - - - - -

BITS WITH EXPLODING PELLETS

Secure from your joke and trick shop some Atom Pearls. These explode when your foot is applied to them. Here are two real cute ways to use them.

1. Place pellet secretly under your foot and ask someone at the table for a match. When you receive matches, look at spectator, and ask: "These are not the kind that explode, are they?" When he says no, say okay and proceed to light match. Look at it for a moment and then light cigarette. Just as flame touches cigarette, step down on pellet. Watch them jump.

2. Again secretly get a pellet under your foot, and
during a dice trick, or just bring out a pair of dice,
and ask if they have seen loaded dice. When they say
" no ", roll the dice out on the table, at the same time
stepping down on the pellet. " They're really loaded! "

— — —

BENT PINS

This is an excellent finish
for the current popular
trick, The Linking Pins.

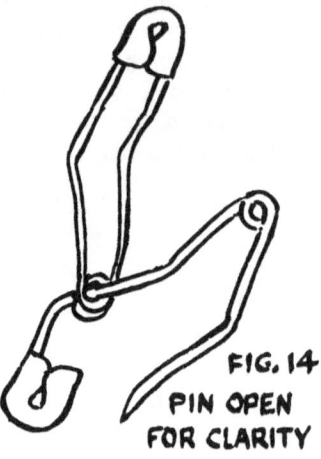

FIG. 14

PIN OPEN

FOR CLARITY

The performer has been
linking and unlinking pins,
in the manner of Piff Paff
Poof, or the Linking Pins.
He then explains that he can
do the trick blindfolded and
to prove this, he places the
pins behind his back.

After a short time, the aud-
ience can see he's having a difficult time of it, whereby
the magician brings the pins to the front where they
are seen to be all twisted out of shape.

Performer claims that he can still do the effect, and
asks spectator to open pins and separate them, so he
can start over. When spectator tries to open pins, he
finds he cannot, for it seems that one of the pins has
become linked on the back bar of the other pin.

It is quite funny to see their expression when they
open the pins and find them locked together. To make
a set of the pins, get two large pins to match your regular set and a pair of pliers. First bend both pins as
in figure 14. Then pry off, very carefully, the head of
one of the pins. Now place the backbar of this pin thru
the small end hole of the other pin. Then replace the
head of pin. Thus both pins will be twisted and locked
together, even when opened.

These two bent pins are under the belt at the back and
are switched when you put the two regular pins behind
your back. You have all the time in the world to do this,
as you want it to look clumsy.

38

READING PALMS

When someone asks if I read
palms, I say yes and
pull out a small rubber
hand and read from it.
" Once upon a time
there was a beautiful..."
(you won't have to go any
further.)

FIG. 15

Just a large rubber doll's
hand and have printed in ink
the above lines. Finish by
saying: " I think the movie
was better."

- - - - -

FLASH STRING IDEAS.

(Reprinted from the New Phoenix)

Here are some ideas using Flash String, just recently
put on the market. Give these a try and you'll find
them very impressive to your audience.

No.1. If you have a little Lippincott coin box, this will
be perfect. The box was made so that a coin could be
inserted into the box while it is locked by a tiny padlock.
The effect was very good, but the search for the little
key and the unlocking took too much time. Now by dis-
carding the lock and tying a short piece of flash string
into a bow about the hasp, the effect is very pretty. After the coin has been inserted into the box, it is taken
from the pocket and handed to a spectator to hold. The
coin (?) is now vanished and you hand a match to the
spectator.

Have him light same and touch to the string where it
disappears in a flash. A line here might possibly be:
" How many safes have you opened this way?" Now the
box is opened and the coin disclosed. Anything using a
lock may be replaced with the string tying idea.

No.2. Try this with your favorite string puzzle. I use
the little puzzle with the small four inch loop. This is

taken by holding it with the two index fingers. The string is now revolved forward, the two index fingers are put together as the two thumbs are placed together and the loop of string is released.

If you don't know the above gag, you can use your own favorite string puzzle. Only a finish is used with the flash string. Have two pieces of string, one regular and one of flash string. Perform the puzzle with the flash string and give the regular piece to the specta- tor. After teaching the spectator how to do the trick, tell him he has only to learn the finish. After perform- ing the string trick, drop the string into an ashtray where a cigarette is burning. The string will disap- pear in a flash. The spectator will go crazy trying to get his string to vanish.

No. 3. This is the real Jim Dandy of the group. Try this and you will really like it. Required is a piece of flash string 18 inches long and a stripper deck. Have card selected in the usual manner and have it returned reversed as per the working of a stripper deck. Have the spectator shuffle the pack (overhand shuffle).Take back the pack and proceed to wrap the pack with the string as you would wrap a package.

Finish by tying with a bow knot, which should be on the bottom, or the card facing out. Now hold the pack with the right thumb and right forefinger at the sides of the pack, so that these fingers come in contact with the protruding s elected card. Have the string touched off with a lit cigarette. The string will disappear and the cards will all drop to the table except the selected card which you will still be holding. This is a pretty way of disclosing a selected card.

It can also be performed with a regular deck by bringing the selected card to the top of the pack and when the string is lit, merely hold on to the top card.

- - -

SADDLE BAGS FOR CLOSE UP WORKERS

This is merely an aid to get your props to the table neatly and quietly.

Two saddle type cloth bags are joined together with

a strip of cloth, so that when
placed on a chair, the performer can sit down, with a bag
hanging on each side of the
chair, to be worked out of.

Excellent for tricks like the
cups and balls and other tricks
that require large apparatus,
like loads, etc.

FIG. 16

- - - - - -

LIFESAVERS AND YOUR QUARTER STACK

It may be news to you to know that Lifesavers (mints)
will fit perfectly into your quarter stack, in lieu of
the traditional pennies or the dice in my version, ear-
lier in this book. This provides you with a good tag
line: " Sure a Life Saver -- the whole trick worked! "

- - - - - -

RUSS WALSH PRODUCTION TABLE BIT

(Reprinted from The New Phoenix)

Secure a cover from one of the " Do It Yourself" books
and have it large enough to cover the folded Walsh Production Table. I made one so that it covers the table
completely. This is now fastened to the top of the table.

To perform, enter with the cover facing your audience.
Explain that you think the Do It Yourself trend is wonderful. Show the cover and say that in this book it explains how to make a table in nothing flat. All that is
needed is a top, a few pieces of metal and it only takes
a few seconds to assemble.

(Here you produce table. In case you do not know, the
Walsh Production Table is a new item by Russ Walsh,
a practical and usable table that folds up small enough
to fit under the coat.)

IT'S A SMALL WORLD

(A World of Gags, reprinted from The New Phoenix)

Go to a school supply department and get a little metal globe of the world with a pencil sharpener in it. Mine is 1 3/4 inches round. With this you can have many laughs. Below are a few I have been using. Remove the pencil sharpener and try these bits of business.

1. Ask a friend how to get to a certain point (maybe a suburb). When he starts to explain, take the globe from your pocket and say: "Here, maybe you can show me exactly how to get there. And don't kid me - I know that blue stuff is water."

2. Since the ball is hollow, with a small round opening, use this in a sponge ball routine. After performing your routine, secure the globe in the left hand. Take the last remaining sponge and push it into your left fist (pushing it into the globe). Say: "Wait until you see the finish. It's out of this world" and produce the globe.

3. When talking to folks it sometimes develops that you know the same people. You can then produce the globe and say: "It certainly is a small world."

4. Lean forward to your best girl (or somebody's best girl), and show globe and say: "Let me take you away from all this."

5. When someone asks: "Where do you live" take out the globe and show them.

- - - - - -

BOWL OR CUP LOAD

This was originally designed to use with my bowl routine. But it, of course, can be adapted to the cups and balls. Here, for explanation, I will describe the effect with the bowl.

The performer has been working the bowl routine and sponges on a paper napkin, which has been opened out on the table. At the finish the bowl is placed mouth down on the napkin and the four corners are folded up over the bowl, which is now inverted on the table.

The illustration shows this. The weight of the bowl plus the fact that the corners are tucked under the bowl, keep the mouth of the bowl like a simple drum head.

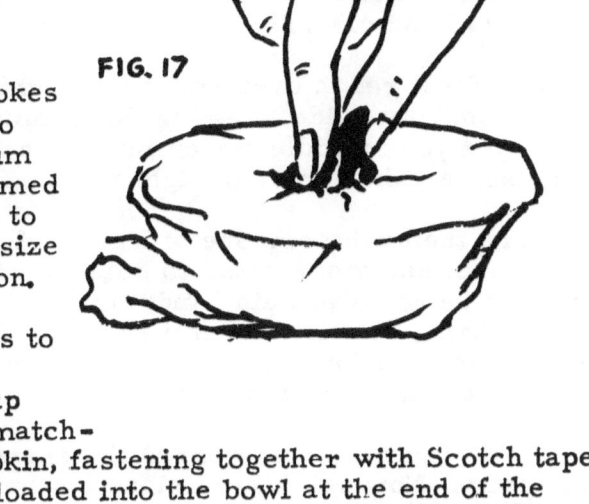

FIG. 17

Performer pokes his finger into the paper drum head thus formed and proceeds to make a good size silk production.

The method is to fold all your silks and wrap them with a matching paper napkin, fastening together with Scotch tape. This is then loaded into the bowl at the end of the routine, the corners folded over as explained and the bowl turned up and proceed to make your silk production.

When you have produced the last silk, take all the napkin pieces, tearing from the bowl the inner napkin which held the silk, together with the outside one and wad up and throw aside.

- - - - - - -

ASHES..........

This excellent impromptu effect has never appeared in print, to my knowledge. It was first shown to me by an excellent close up man, Jim Ryan of Chicago.

Effect: The performer asks someone to light a cigarette and then asks another assistant spectator to hold out his right hand, palm down. The performer requests spectator to close his hand tightly into a fist. The magician then asks for the cigarette just lit and proceeds to knock off a few of the ashes on the back of the spectator's closed fist. These are then rubbed into the skin, and the magician lights a match and passes it around the closed fist. Asking if he felt anything, the spectator replies: "No."

Performer then has spectator open his hand and there in the palm of his hand, the spectator finds the ashes. The magician then hands the spectator a handkerchief to wipe his hand clean.

Method: First reach over with your right hand and move an ashtray aside. During this moment, you contrive to put your middle finger into the ashtray, thus getting some ashes on your right middle finger.

Pause and then ask someone to light a cigarette. When this is done, ask a spectator to hold out his hand palm down. As he holds out his hand, quickly take it with the right hand, secretly touching the spectator's palm with your middle finger as you push his hand back, saying: "No, hold it closer to you."

In this way you have transferred the smear of ashes to his palm. Now ask him to close his hand into a fist. They will never remember you even touching the hand. Now proceed as above and when you rub the ashes into the back of spectator's hand, do this with your middle finger of your right hand, thus destroying the remaining ashes on your finger.

If you can, work this on a lady spectator. It is amazing how simple the method is and how strong the effect.

- - - - - -

BILL,LEMON AND WRAPPER

This is a variation of the Bill in Lemon trick, based on the little known fact that a lemon wrapper when lit with a match will burn and float, as in the Red Ashes trick. With this little wrinkle in mind, the following effect can be presented.

Effect: The performer displays a lemon wrapped in paper. He borrows a bill and has the last four numbers recorded by a spectator. The lemon is then unwrapped and given to a spectator to hold, and the bill is rolled up and placed in the middle of the paper wrapper. It is then twisted around the bill and lit with a cigarette lighter. The paper burns and then suddenly floats up into the air.

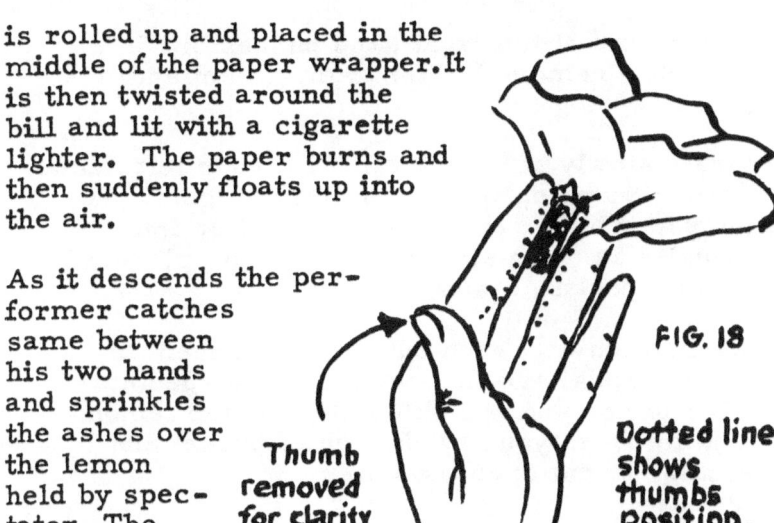

FIG. 18

As it descends the per-former catches same between his two hands and sprinkles the ashes over the lemon held by spec-tator. The spectator is then requested

Thumb removed for clarity

Dotted line shows thumbs position.

to cut open the lemon and inside is found the bill, the last four numbers are verified , and the bill is returned to its owner.

Preparation: Remove the pip from the lemon and carefully insert a rolled up bill, from which you have the last four numbers memorized. I usually wrap the bill in a small piece of Sarran Wrap, so as to keep the bill nice and dry. Now replace the pip of the lemon and glue this into place with a small dab of airplane glue. When dry, rewrap the lemon in wrapper and with a cigarette in your left coat pocket you are ready --

To perform: Display the lemon wrapped and place on table. Proceed to borrow a bill, and when you re-ceive same, ask someone to write down the last four numbers of the serial number. You call out the num-bers previously memorized, and these will later be verified. (You may wish to do the torn corner bit, too).

Now proceed to fold the bill into quarters and then roll this into a little tube, tightly as possible. With your right hand pick up lemon and shake same out of paper wrapper into a spectator's hand, and then take bill and place into center of paper. Put it at right angles to the wrapper, and as you do so, push the tip of the rolled up bill right thru the paper and im-mediately fold paper around bill. As you twist the paper, the thumb of the right hand pushes bill into left hand. Now remove lighter from pocket and light the paper.

As it burns, slowly pull back bill with your left thumb and as paper burns down to your fingers, gently re-lease the paper ashes and they will float up into the air. Casually as you watch paper float up, place your left hand into pocket, disposing of bill.

As ashes float down, reach out and catch them in your cupped hands, and then walk over to spectator holding the lemon and sprinkle ashes on the lemon. Remove knife from your handkerchief pocket and ask spectator to cut open the lemon.

He does this and discovers the bill. Now unwrap the bill and have the numbers verified. Bow and exit with the borrowed bill, if you can get away with it.

The cut lemon may now be used to remove tobacco stains from your fingers. Why waste it?

- - - - -

A DARKER SHADE OF MALINI

The production of an item has always seemed to me the most effective trick you can do close-up. Partic-ularly if the item is unusual. The Malini Brick trick has always appealed to me, and after doing this for a while, I hit on a variation which I hope you will like. It is something people will talk about and remember you for a long time.

Effect: The performer (that's you) removes from his pocket a dime and a penny. Also a fez, which has been folded into a compact bundle. This will later remind them that the production item couldn't have been hidden in the fez from the beginning.

The magician places the dime and penny on the table and covers them with the fez. He explains the object of the trick is to cause the dime to vanish. On lifting the fez, the dime HAS disappeared. He now ex-plains that the penny will vanish.

On lifting the fez, the penny is still on the table.

Apparently confusion has taken place. Suddenly re-
membering, perfor-
mer explains that the
penny is supposed to
be placed into his
pocket and have it
return magically
under the fez.

FIG.19

He places penny in
his pocket and says
the magic words:
Lincoln Blinken and
asks spectator to lift
fez.

When spectator lifts
fez, a lump of coal is
seen in the middle of
the table. Take my
word for it, this hits
them right between the eyes. Now for the

Method: Secure a fez, the Shriner type, only undec-
orated. Roll this up and place in the inside coat pocket. Also a dime and penny trick will be needed. Now
go out and steal a lump of coal that will fit into the
fez. When you have one the right size, get from your
paint store some Krylon plastic clear spray paint.

Proceed to spray the lump of coal. Give it four or
five coats. This will prevent it from soiling things
and also makes it a bit easier to handle. Now the
problem is to get the lump of coal to the table.

This is my method. Others may come to you. I do
the Monkey in the Basket trick, so I always come to
the table with the basket. This also holds my other
props. So I load the lump of coal into the basket and
as I set it on the floor, I remove the lump and place
it between my knees.

You will now be ready to proceed.

To perform: Remove the dime and penny gimmick
from your pocket and place them on the table, the
penny overlapping the dime. Remove the fez and

47

and unroll it, and display same by pinching it from above. Explain that the object of the trick is to cause the dime to vanish.

As you cover the dime and penny with the fez, held in the right hand, your left hand, which has been resting on the two coins pushes them together. Say the magic words and get the lump of coal into your left hand for loading into the fez.

Slowly lift the fez up and toward you, and as the attention is on the penny, load in the lump of coal. Replace the fez over the penny and explain that the object of the trick now is to cause the penny to vanish. Lift up the fez with the right hand and show that the penny is still there.

It will take a little practice to lift fez as tho it contained nothing, but a few trials will show you how simple it is. Once again cover penny and say: Lincoln Blinken. Slowly lift fez and penny is still there.

Remove penny from table with left hand and replace fez in center of table. Explain that it might be better if you placed penny into your pocket and caused it to return under the fez.

Place penny into your pocket, saying: "Remember the penny is MINE." Ask spectator to lift up fez. As he does this, say: "And that's MINED, too. After all, it may be a cold winter.... "

You may wish to carry the lump of coal to the table, hidden by your coat. No matter how you get it under the table, it will be worth the trouble. And don't forget, it may be a cold winter.....

– – – – –

FINIS

www.ingramcontent.com/pod-product-compliance
Lightning Source LLC
Chambersburg PA
CBHW022156260626
47155CB00018B/2265